CAR TRAVEL GAMES

Tony Potter

Edited by Jenny Tyler

Designed by Tony Potter

**Illustrated by Iain Ashman
and Chris Lyon**

Additional illustrations by Guy Smith

Contents
2 Playing travel games
4 Journey log
6 Games and puzzles
30 Answers

With thanks to Books at Home

Playing travel games

There are lots of games, puzzles and activities in this book. Some can be played on your own, but others are for teams. More than one person is needed whenever you see this picture symbol:

You can score points in lots of the games. You might like to make a score card, like the one shown on the right, so that you can see who is the overall winner at the end of a journey. It is a good idea to ask one person to keep the scores and be referee. The referee is in charge and decides how many points each person scores. Games with scores have this picture symbol:

It helps to have a pencil and paper handy for some of the games and puzzles. These are essential when you see this picture symbol:

Most of the games can be altered to suit your journey. For example, there are lists of things to spot which you can change to suit motorway rather than town driving.

You can play many of the games and solve the puzzles at home. Some have special rules to follow if you want to do this.

You will find answers to all the puzzles on pages 30 to 32.

It is very dangerous for drivers to take their eyes off the road. They can join in some games safely, but may not want to play at all, so it is best not to bother them by keep asking. Try not to distract the driver by moving about or making too much noise.

GAME	AUNTY ETHEL	SPIKE (THE DOG)	GRUMPY GRANDPA	ME
Collector's quest	10	8	9	10
Zoo	10	0	0	0
Navigator	5	5	0	0
Missing Parts	3	3	2	12
Memory car	12	10	5	10
TOTAL	40	26	16	32

WINNER : Aunty Ethel ← with help from me

For some games you might find it helpful for each person to keep a tally of their score, like this:

1 Draw a line for each point scored, up to four, like this: ||||

2 Then draw another line to show you have five points, like this: ‖‖

3 Carry on scoring in chunks of five points. This makes it easy to add the scores at the end of the game. ‖‖ ‖‖ ‖‖ ‖‖ ||| = 23

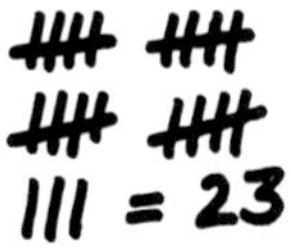

Things to take

You need to take these things with you to be able to play the games. It is a good idea to read this book before leaving, as there are some things to make which are easier to do at home.

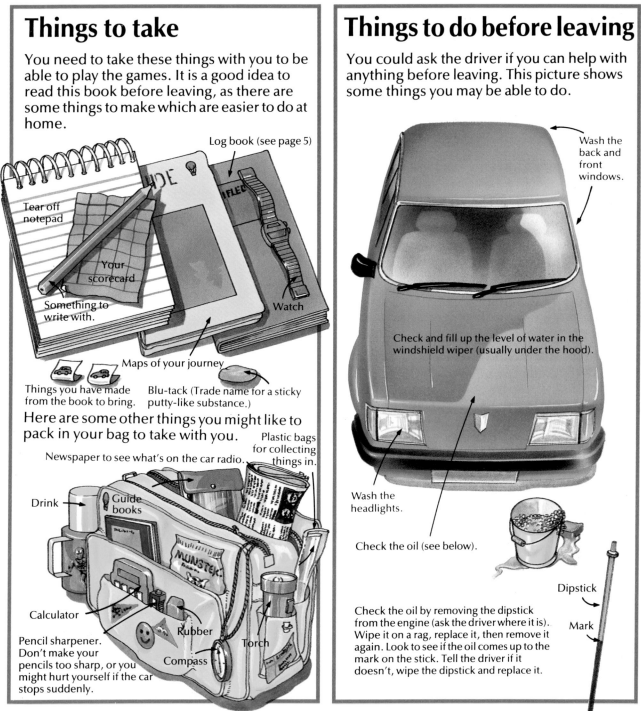

Log book (see page 5)

Tear off notepad

Your scorecard

Something to write with.

Watch

Maps of your journey

Things you have made from the book to bring.

Blu-tack (Trade name for a sticky putty-like substance.)

Here are some other things you might like to pack in your bag to take with you.

Newspaper to see what's on the car radio.

Plastic bags for collecting things in.

Drink

Guide books

Calculator

Pencil sharpener. Don't make your pencils too sharp, or you might hurt yourself if the car stops suddenly.

Rubber

Torch

Compass

Things to do before leaving

You could ask the driver if you can help with anything before leaving. This picture shows some things you may be able to do.

Wash the back and front windows.

Check and fill up the level of water in the windshield wiper (usually under the hood).

Wash the headlights.

Check the oil (see below).

Dipstick

Mark

Check the oil by removing the dipstick from the engine (ask the driver where it is). Wipe it on a rag, replace it, then remove it again. Look to see if the oil comes up to the mark on the stick. Tell the driver if it doesn't, wipe the dipstick and replace it.

Journey log

Before setting off you could make a journey log, like the one shown opposite, to record details of your journey. The picture below explains the instruments you're likely to find on the car dashboard to help fill in some of the details on your log. All cars vary, so ask the driver where the instruments are in your car.

Dashboard instruments

1 **Speedometer** – shows the car's speed, usually both in kilometers per hour (kph) and miles per hour (mph).

2 **Odometer** – shows how far the car has been driven since it was made.

3 **Trip counter** – shows how far the car has been on a particular journey. Ask the driver to set this before leaving.

4 **Tachometer** – tells the speed of the engine in thousands of revolutions per minute. This often looks like the speedometer, so ask the driver which is which as you don't need to use this one. Not all cars have them.

5 **Gas gauge** – shows how much gas is in the tank. They are usually marked so you can see if the tank is full, ¾ full, ½ full or empty. Ask the driver how much gas the tank holds when full. You can then work out roughly how much gas is in the tank. Or, if the driver fills up with gas when the tank is empty, you can see how much has been put in by looking at the gas pump.

Making the log

It is a good idea to make your journey log in a separate book. You can then make a new log for each journey and keep a record of everywhere you go. After a year you could work out how many towns you have passed through, how far you have travelled and so on. Make your log like this:

1 Draw lines to divide the pages up into three boxes; the top for when you set off, the middle for the journey, and the bottom for when you arrive.

2 Divide up the boxes as shown. For the middle section you will need to look at a map to see how many towns you expect to pass through, and to work out places of interest on the route.

3 Fill-in the details as you go.

Amount of gas in tank	6 gallons		Odometer reading	035355	Departure time	9.30 a.m.
			Trip reading	00000	Weather	Rain

Towns passed through. (Tick when spotted)		Places of interest (Tick when spotted)	
CASTLETOWN	✓	BIGDROP CASTLE	✓
SPLASHRIVER FALLS	✓	OLD RUINS	✓
FALLOVER DOWNS	✓	NATURE PARK	✓
TIMBERFELLS	✓	GREENTOP FOREST	✓
STEAMVILLE	✓	OLD RAILWAY STATION	✓
NOTQUITA CITY	✓	AIRPORT	✓
ALMOSTHERE TOWN	✓	AUNTY FLO'S HOUSE	✓
GORILLATON	✓	NATURE PARK	✓

Distance Travelled	Time	Weather
2 miles	9.35	Rain
8 miles	9.45	Rain
14 miles	10.00	Rain
32 miles	10.25	Still. Raining!
41 miles	10.40	Stopped raining!
42 miles	10.45	Cloudy
47 miles	10.55	Sunny— at last!
49 miles	11.00	Still Sunny!

Time of arrival	11.00 a.m.
Total journey time	1½ hours
Odometer reading	035404
Trip reading	00049
Amount of gas used	3 gallons

Average gas consumption (Divide distance travelled by amount of gas used)	16 miles per gallon
Average speed (Divide distance travelled by time taken)	32 miles per hour

Treasure hunt

Ivan Engine (in the red car) and Dora Handel (in the yellow car) have the clues below, directing them to a hoard of treasure buried somewhere on the map. They are told to fill their gas tanks at the nearest garage before setting off, and to drive at the same speed. the clues to work out where the treasure is. Then measure their journeys to see who gets there first. Look at the red box if you are not sure how to do this.

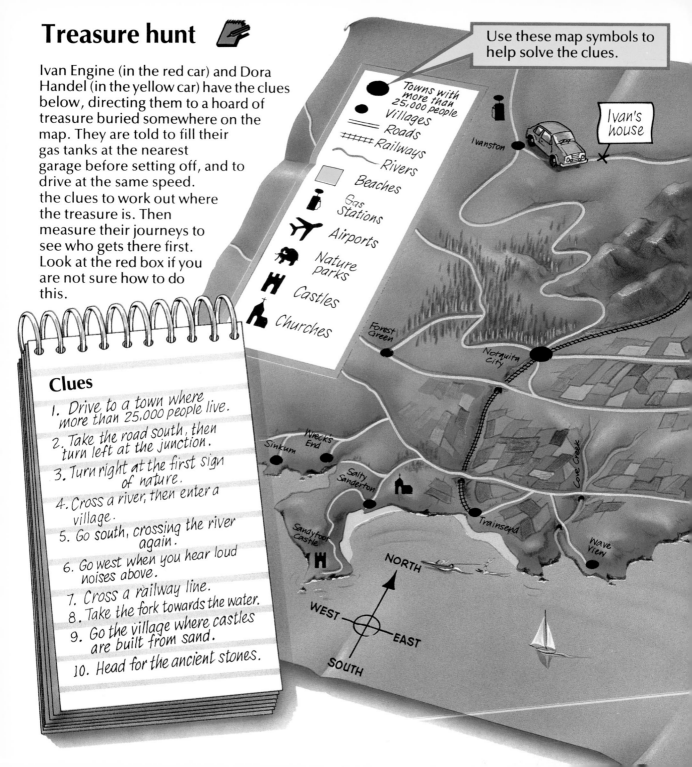

Use these map symbols to help solve the clues.

● Towns with more than 25,000 people
● Villages
= Roads
╫╫╫ Railways
~ Rivers
▢ Beaches
⌷ Gas Stations
✈ Airports
🐘 Nature parks
♜ Castles
⛪ Churches

Ivan's house

Ivanston

Forest Green

Norquita City

Sinkum

Wreck's End

Salty Sanderton

Sandyfoot Castle

Trainsend

Cove Creek

Wave View

NORTH
WEST — EAST
SOUTH

Clues

1. Drive to a town where more than 25,000 people live.
2. Take the road south, then turn left at the junction.
3. Turn right at the first sign of nature.
4. Cross a river, then enter a village.
5. Go south, crossing the river again.
6. Go west when you hear loud noises above.
7. Cross a railway line.
8. Take the fork towards the water.
9. Go the village where castles are built from sand.
10. Head for the ancient stones.

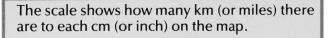
The scale shows how many km (or miles) there are to each cm (or inch) on the map.

```
        0
        MILES         10                    20                    30
    ┌─────────────────────────────────────────────────────────────────────────┐
    │ KM                                                                    40  │
    │  0    10    20    30    40    50    60    70    80    90    100           │
    └─────────────────────────────────────────────────────────────────────────┘
```

Mountainsville Heights

Doraville

Dora's house

Fallover Downs

Lake Smellie

Gorillaton

River Smellie

Swimmalot Cliffs

Deepwater

Cove Castle

Castle Falls

Ivan and Dora

Here are some other questions.

How far is it from Dora's house to the treasure?

How far is it from Ivan's house to the treasure?

How many rivers does Ivan cross on his journey?

Dora's car does 20 miles per gallon. Ivan's car only does 15 miles per gallon. See if you can work out who used most gas finding the treasure.

Measuring distances

The steps below show how to find out actual distances between two points on a map.

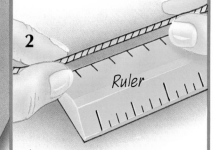

1

Thread

▲
Hold a piece of thread along the line of the road between the points you want to measure.

2

Ruler

▲
Hold the thread tight against the scale of the map or a ruler to measure the distance in cm or inches.

Actual distance = length of thread × number of km (or miles) in one cm (or inch).

Secret agent

James Pond, secret agent, is at a garage 90 miles from safety over the border in Venuzlulu. S.Q.U.A.S.H. agents are 30 miles behind, driving at 90 mph. James buys a getaway car, but it has a slight fault. See if you can work out which car he buys to escape from the enemy in time. Hint: work out how long the agents take to get to the border, then how long each car would take.

This car is so rusty that its floor will drop out if driven faster than 90 mph.

The jeep only has reverse gear, but goes backwards at 62 mph.

Border
VENUZLULU
150km (90 miles)
James Pond
50 km (30 miles)
S.Q.U.A.S.H. Agents

Signpost 卌

Tara Mack puts up seven of the warning signs on the right on the planet Auto, at the places shown by the numbered triangles. See if you can write a list of the signs she takes, in the order she puts them up. Match the letter beside the signs with the number in the triangles.

Tara Mack

A   B   C   D

E   F   G   H

1   2   3

The blue car does 30 mph. Its radiator leaks, though, and after half an hour the engine overheats and stops.

The orange pick-up does 90 mph, but needs new spark plugs every 15 minutes. These take 10 minutes to fit.

◄ The red sports car does 180 mph, but its gas tank leaks and is empty after 20 minutes.

How far?

This blue car takes three minutes at 20 mph to reach the top of the hill and three minutes at twice the speed to reach the bottom. How far has it travelled?

Did you know?

There are over 400 million cars in the world – a third in the USA. If every car were parked bumper to bumper, they would go round the equator 41 times.

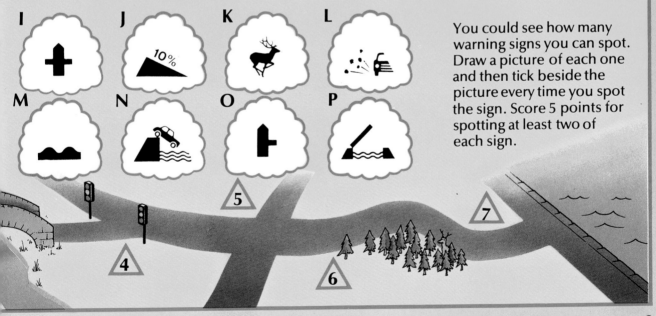

I J K L

M N O P

You could see how many warning signs you can spot. Draw a picture of each one and then tick beside the picture every time you spot the sign. Score 5 points for spotting at least two of each sign.

Cops and robbers

Split into two teams – cops and robbers. The cops want to catch the robbers, but five oil drums block the way. The robbers can't escape because their tires are all punctured (including the spare). Take turns to ask the other team questions, using those below, or ideas of your own. For each correct answer the cops remove an oil drum or the robbers mend a puncture. The cops make an arrest by removing all the oil drums, but the robbers escape by mending all the punctures.

Did you know?

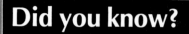

If all the car tires in the world (not including spares) were piled up, they would make a column two thirds of the way to the moon.

Bus stop

Split into two teams and each take one side of the road. Count the number of people waiting at bus stops on your side. The first team to count to 100 wins.

Questions

Which city is the capital of Norway?

How long is a decade?

Where would you see the Mona Lisa?

Who said, "Elementary my dear Watson?"

Where do Maoris live?

What's big and red and eats rocks?

What's 7 × 9?

What's odd about the buses in Venice?

How long is a piece of string?

Keep your score on a piece of paper.

Legs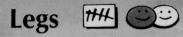

Split into two teams. Each team has to count the number of legs on one side of the road, including bench legs, dogs' legs, statue legs and so on. The winning team is the first to reach 100.

How many legs did the teams in the red car count? Score 5 points for the right answer.

Tunnel

Aver is 20 miles from Lanch by mountain road and 10 miles using the tunnel. It takes 10 minutes to line up for the tunnel. Which is the fastest route driving at 40mph.

Autogram

HONDA =
Had on

RENAULT
= Late run

Make a list of all the different car and truck names you can think of or spot out of the window. Then try unscrambling them to make new words like those above.

Who lives there?

Take turns to describe the owners of unusual houses seen on your journey. Imagine what they look like, their favorite food, the pets they keep and so on.

Antennas and Mufflers

This game is for two players. Hold the book between you. Put your finger on one of the start spots. As soon as you see a car out of the window of the same color as an antenna leading from the start spot, trace with your finger up the antenna to the next spot. Wait until you see another car. You then go up antennas or down mufflers, from spot to spot, according to the color of the next car you see. The first to reach the gas pump is the winner.

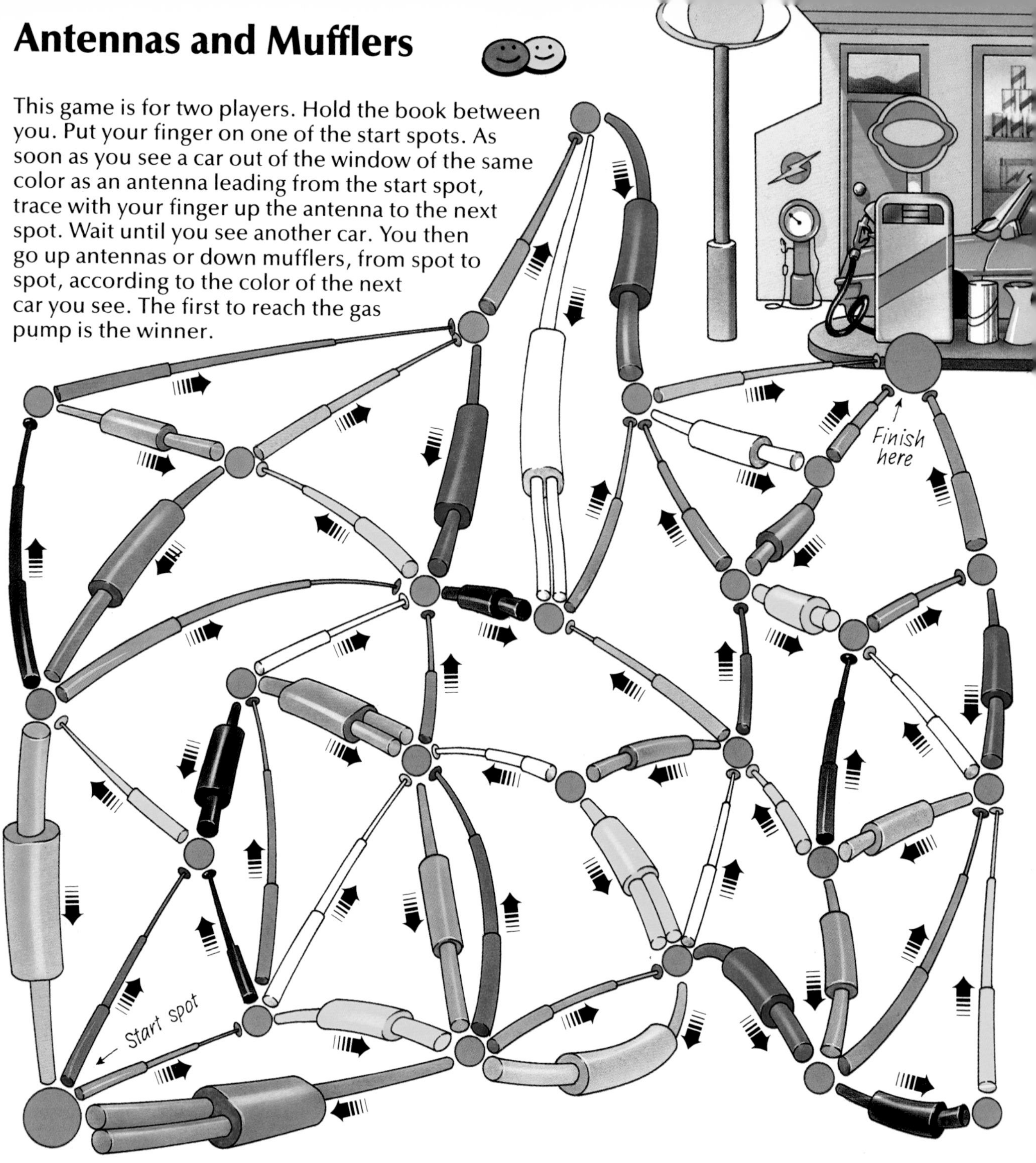

Finish here

Start spot

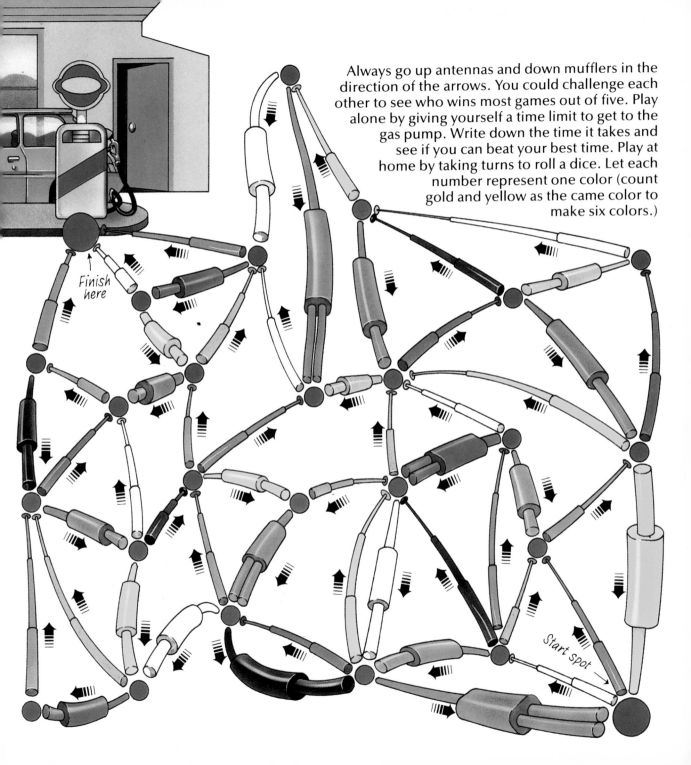

Always go up antennas and down mufflers in the direction of the arrows. You could challenge each other to see who wins most games out of five. Play alone by giving yourself a time limit to get to the gas pump. Write down the time it takes and see if you can beat your best time. Play at home by taking turns to roll a dice. Let each number represent one color (count gold and yellow as the came color to make six colors.)

Finish here

Start spot

Fred's car

Fred's car uses all the parts below after the distances shown. He pays for them in car keys where he lives (on the planet Auto). See if you can work out Fred's bill, in car keys, after driving 60,000 miles.

Two fan belts every 12,000 miles.
Price: two keys each.

Six spark plugs every 3,000 miles.
Price: 5 keys each.

One air filter every 6,000 miles.
Price: 1 key each.

One can of oil every 3,000 miles.
Price: 10 keys a can.

Three tires every 6,000 miles.
Price: 20 keys each.

Navigator

Mark Skidd decided to visit his Aunty on the other side of town. Before setting off he made a chart like the one below. In each column he wrote a guess of how many times he would go round a roundabout, turn left, right or go through traffic lights. He then kept a count of how often he actually made these movements on the journey.

Mark Skidd's house

Car parked here

Aunty's house

Mark parks here

Mark drove to his Aunty's by the shortest route. How many times did he guess his movements correctly?

Make a chart like Mark's for your own journey and score five points for each correct guess you make.

Hint: Look at a map before leaving to work out the movements you might make.

MOVEMENTS	ROUND ABOUTS	LEFT TURNS	RIGHT TURNS	TRAFFIC LIGHTS
GUESSES	2	2	9	4
ACTUAL MOVEMENTS	?	?	?	?

Pink toads

What do you eat for breakfast?

Take turns to ask each other silly questions. The answer must always be, "Pink toads". You're out if you laugh when you answer. The winner is the last person left.

Quick games ⊞

1 Everyone (except the driver) shuts their eyes and listens to the car. After a while, the driver asks what the car's speed is. The nearest answer scores 5 points.

2 Take turns to guess the colour of the next car to come round a bend. Score 1 point if you guess correctly.

3 Play "car spy" (like "I spy"). Start with, "I spy with my little eye, a car beginning with . . ." Use the first letter of car names you see.

Did you know?

The first car radio in the world was fitted to a Ford Model T in 1922 by a driver in Chicago, USA.

Missing parts ⊞

A mechanic re-built these old cars, but forgot at least 16 things from the one on the right.

Score one point for each missing part you find.

15

Destination

This game is for two players, starting at opposite ends of the road. The winner is the first to get to the other end. Make the counters shown below, before leaving home, and use Blu-tack* to stick them to the book.

Take turns to spot things from the chart opposite to move your counter along the road. You must move the number of squares shown beside each thing. If you land on a white square, your next move must be in the direction shown by the arrow.

How to make counters

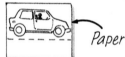

Paper

For each counter, trace this picture on paper and glue it to thin card.

Card

Cut round here

Scissors

Colour the car, then cut as shown.

Bend here

Blu-tack

Bend the counter along the dotted line so it stands up. Then stick a piece of Blu-tack* underneath.

Go straight through tunnels to get to the other side of the page.

Player 1 starts here

*Blu-tack is the trade name for a sticky putty used to hang posters on the wall.

Player 2 starts here

Score chart

Truck = 1

Speed sign = 2

30

Horse = 3

Bridge = 4

Church = 5

Telephone = 6

You could make a different spotting chart to suit your journey.

You could play this game at home using a dice to make the moves.

17

Zoo

The idea of this game is to be first to collect 20 "animals" for a zoo. First write down a list of animals to be captured by spotting certain things out of the window. The notepad on the right gives some ideas – a park bench could count as an elephant, a policeman as a tiger and so on. Everyone has to use the same list and remember what's on it.

You capture an "animal" by being first to spot it and call out its name. It escapes if you call it by the wrong name, but can be captured by someone else. The first person to fill their zoo scores 10 points.

Escape

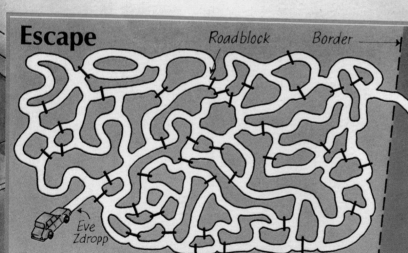

Eve Zdropp, the spy, is trying to escape from the police. Unfortunately, they seem to have set-up road blocks everywhere. But there is one route to safety across the border – can you find it?

Did you know?

Nearly 20 million Volkswagon Beetles have been produced. 50,007 football fields would be needed to park them all at once.

18

Number cruncher

Look out of one side of the car and spot as many numbers as you can. You have to add each individual digit in your head until you get to 100. Zeros don't count. You could challenge someone else to look out of the other side of the car and see who gets to 100 first.

Who has added the largest number in the blue car? Score 5 points for the correct answer.

AVER 69

LANCH 89

82

30

8.56
2.62

OPEN UNTIL 8.30

Memory car

Look at this picture of car parts for 30 seconds and then close the book. In two minutes write down as many things as you can remember. Score 1 point for each correct item, but lose 2 points for any you get wrong.

19

Word race

This game is for up to five players. Make counters as shown on page 16 – one for each driver. Choose one of the lanes at the start of the track and stick your counter to the blue square with Blu-tack.

Look for words on signs out of the car window. When you spot a word beginning with the

letter on the diamond in front of you, move your counter forwards to the next blue section of your lane.

At the same time, you can (if you want to) move sideways in the new section across one of the orange diamonds, to put your counter in a different lane.

By doing this you will be able to block the path of another driver, as only one driver at a time is allowed on a blue square.

The winner is the first to get to the finish line.

Start on one of these squares.

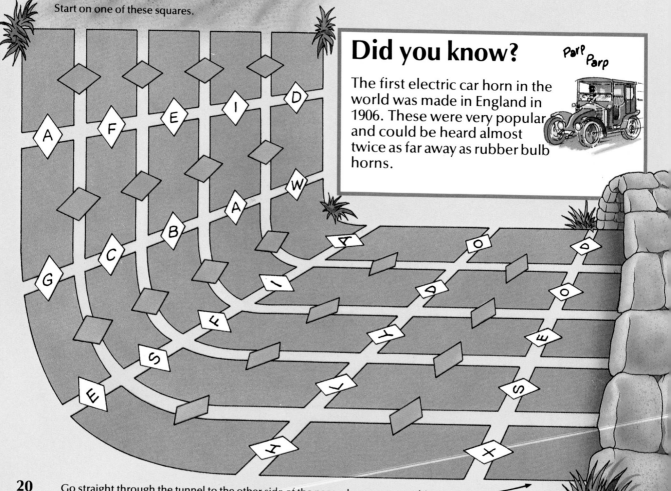

Did you know?

Parp Parp

The first electric car horn in the world was made in England in 1906. These were very popular and could be heard almost twice as far away as rubber bulb horns.

20   Go straight through the tunnel to the other side of the page when you get to this row.

Funny maps

Place a pad of paper on your knee and hold a blunt pencil over the paper without it touching. As you go over bumps, the pencil will touch the paper and draw a funny map. You could color in your map when you stop for a break.

Signpost

Everyone has to guess how long it will take to get from one signpost to the next. Write your guesses down and time how long it actually takes using a watch. The person with the nearest guess scores 1 point.

You could decide to do more than one lap of the race. Go back to the start line when you get to the end if you want to do this.

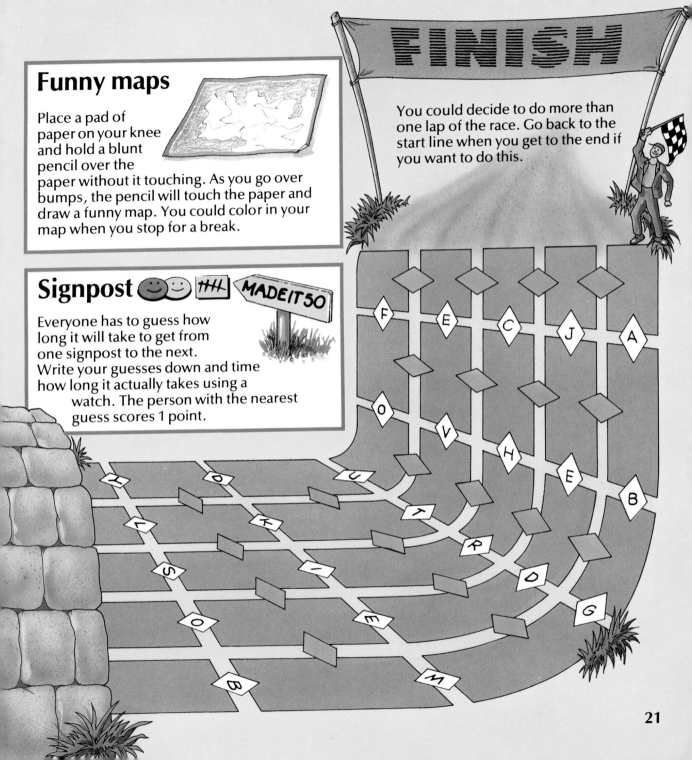

21

Collector's quest

Make a list of ten things to collect and bring home from an outing. Try to think of things likely to be found at your destination, but don't include anything too large to fit in the car. Score 5 points for each item you collect.

Look at this beach scene to see how many things you can spot from the list below. Score 1 point for every item you find.

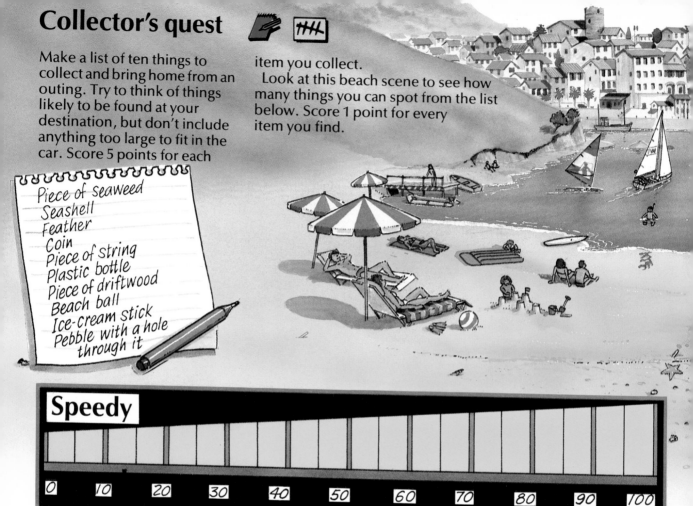

Piece of seaweed
Seashell
Feather
Coin
Piece of string
Plastic bottle
Piece of driftwood
Beach ball
Ice-cream stick
Pebble with a hole through it

Speedy

0   10   20   30   40   50   60   70   80   90   100

For this game you need a copy of the speedometer above for each player. You then color it in, 5 or 10 mph at a time, by being first to say "speedy" when you spot something from the charts on the right. The first to reach top speed is the winner.

Spotting these increases your speed by 5kph (or mph).

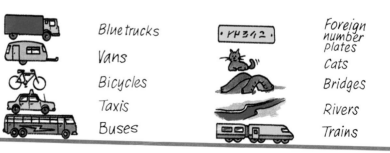

Blue trucks

Vans

Bicycles

Taxis

Buses

Spotting these increases your speed by 10kph (or mph).

· YH342 ·

Foreign number plates

Cats

Bridges

Rivers

Trains

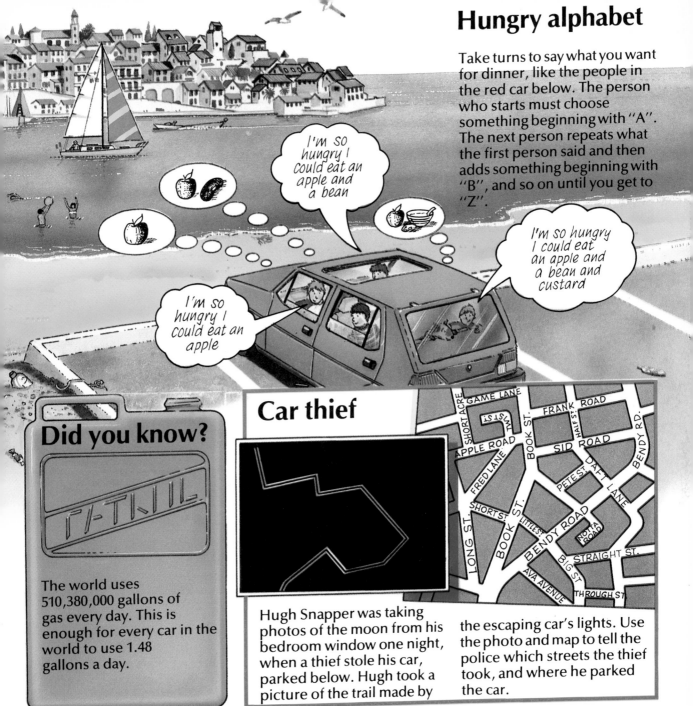

Hungry alphabet

Take turns to say what you want for dinner, like the people in the red car below. The person who starts must choose something beginning with "A". The next person repeats what the first person said and then adds something beginning with "B", and so on until you get to "Z".

I'm so hungry I could eat an apple and a bean

I'm so hungry I could eat an apple and a bean and custard

I'm so hungry I could eat an apple

Did you know?

The world uses 510,380,000 gallons of gas every day. This is enough for every car in the world to use 1.48 gallons a day.

Car thief

Hugh Snapper was taking photos of the moon from his bedroom window one night, when a thief stole his car, parked below. Hugh took a picture of the trail made by the escaping car's lights. Use the photo and map to tell the police which streets the thief took, and where he parked the car.

Hats off

Follow the steps below to make hats for everybody from sheets of newspaper*. Then put them on. The first person to take off their hat the instant they spot someone wearing a hat outside the car scores a point. The winner is the first to score 10 points.

1

Fold the paper in half.

2

Fold two corners over as shown above.

3

Fold both edges

Fold the bottom edge over on each side and press it flat.

4

Open the paper out to make a hat.

Open out here

Delivery

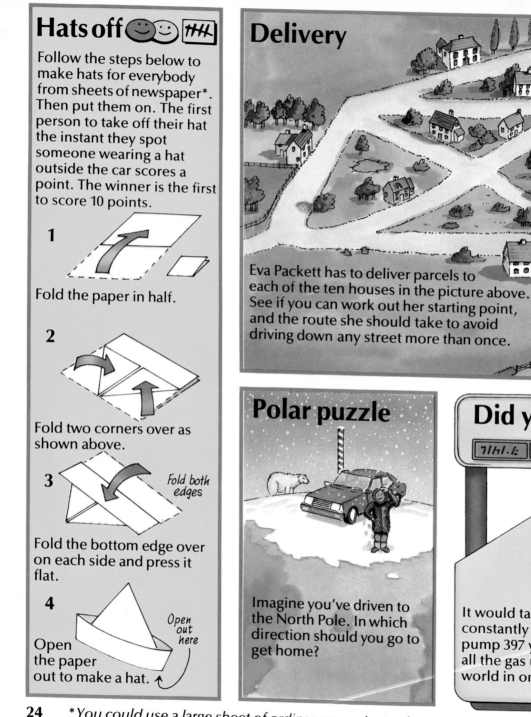

Eva Packett has to deliver parcels to each of the ten houses in the picture above. See if you can work out her starting point, and the route she should take to avoid driving down any street more than once.

Polar puzzle

Imagine you've driven to the North Pole. In which direction should you go to get home?

Did you know?

It would take one constantly running gas pump 397 years to dispense all the gas used in the world in one day.

You could use a large sheet of ordinary paper instead.

Street story

Take turns to make up a funny story using words spotted on street signs, in shop windows, on truck sides and so on.

Look at the picture above and see if you can continue this story:
"Yesterday I walked along Apple Street, met Albert the gorilla and then ate an ice-cream in a bird's nest. Later I . . ."

Insultabot

Choose one person to act as a "robot". Take turns to ask the robot questions about yourself beginning with the words, "Am I . . .?" The robot is allowed to insult you by replying according to the first thing it sees from the chart on the right. You can see how the game works in the picture.

Choose a new robot after an agreed distance. You could write your own list of things to spot with new insults.

Am I clever?

I suppose a gorilla might think so!

Before setting off you could make a mask like this from cardboard for the "robot" to wear.

Insults

=	"I'll only tell you if you get back in your cage!"
=	"Of course you are!"
=	"Take the monster suit off and I might tell you!"
=	"I suppose a gorilla might think so!"
=	"No, you're a slug!"

Plastic or card lids stuck together

Card

Elastic

25

Travel consequences

For this game you need a piece of paper for each player. Start by asking everyone to write a funny name at the top of the paper. Then fold the paper over, to conceal the name, like this:

Pass your paper to the person sitting next to you, so they go round in a circle. Continue by writing things which fit the sequence of phrases shown on the right, folding the papers and passing them round each time.

Went to...

And met...

They said...

And decided to go to...

But, on the way...

So they decided to...

At the end, unfold the papers and read them out, using the words in the speech bubbles to make sentences for each section.

FRED
THE SOUTH POLE
KING KONG
FANCY MEETING YOU HERE
A MOVIE
THEIR CAR BROKE DOWN
GO FISHING INSTEAD

Banana

One person goes to "sleep" by covering their ears and closing their eyes. Then everyone else picks one verb between them. Verbs are "doing" words, like run, jump, sleep, sit, sneeze and so on.

Get the person to "wake up" when the verb has been agreed. They then have to discover the chosen word by asking up to ten questions, changing the verb in the question to, "Banana". For example, they could ask, "Do you banana in the car?", or, "Am I bananaring right now?".

The sleepy person scores 5 points if they guess the verb from 10 or less questions. Then change players.

26

Suitcase

Here are some things you
might like to take on holiday.
Each choose ten things from
the picture and write a list of
your choices. Draw a picture
beside each item, like this:

Teddy bear
Car
Slippers
Beach ball
Bat
Gloves
Socks
Cards
Towel
Hat

To be allowed your choice you
have to spot things beginning
with the same letter (or letters
if the item is two words) and of
the same color. For example,
to take a green pencil you
could spot something like a
green pick-up.

Call, "Suitcase" when you
spot something and tell
everyone what it is so they can
check the spelling and colour.
Then tick the item on your list.

The winner is the first person
to tick everything on their list
and scores 5 points.

27

Duck and jump

Everyone has five "lives". Lift your feet when going over bridges and duck when going under them. You lose a life if you forget. The last person "alive" wins.

East and west

Sid Speedy's car was facing west. After driving for five minutes Sid found that he'd actually gone east. How did this happen?

Where am I?

Play this game on a route you know well. Cover your eyes until the driver calls, "Ready". Then guess where you are. The person with the nearest guess wins.

Road builder

Nine villages in the mountains were cut off from each other until a road builder linked them together. He was told to build four straight stretches of road, but was not allowed to go over or through any mountain. See if you can draw a picture of the route he worked out.

Quick games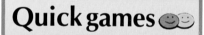

1 Each write down something to spot. Call, "Pairs" each time you see a pair of your things. The winner is the first to spot ten pairs.

2 Guess how many traffic lights out of ten you will be able to go through without having to stop. The winner is the person with the nearest guess.